The
Other

©1995 Alejandro Aura (text)
©1995 Julia Gukova (art)
Design by Julia Gukova
Cover and typography design by Sheryl Shapiro
Translation from the Spanish by Shirley Langer and Sally Stokes Sefami.

Annick Press Ltd.

Original Spanish edition, *El otro lado*, published by
Fondo de Cultura Economica, Mexico. ©1993

Canadian Cataloguing in Publication Data
  Aura, Alejandro
    The other side

  Translation of: El otro lado.
  ISBN 1-55037-405-2

  I. Gukova, Julia. II. Title.

  PZ7.A87Ot 1995   j863   C95-930899-7

The art in this book was rendered in mixed media.
The text was typeset in Schadow and Lucian.

Distributed in Canada by: Published in the U.S.A. by Annick Press (U.S.) Ltd.
Firefly Books Ltd.   Distributed in the U.S.A. by:
250 Sparks Avenue   Firefly Books (U.S.) Inc.
Willowdale, ON   P.O. Box 1338
M2H 2S4   Ellicott Station
                        Buffalo, NY 14205

∞ Printed on acid-free paper.

Printed and bound in Canada by
D.W. Friesen & Sons, Altona, Manitoba

Side

Story by
Alejandro Aura

Illustrated by
Julia Gukova

Annick Press Ltd. • Toronto • New York

One day the king

summoned the **children** of his kingdom and said,

"I want to know what is on The **Other** Side. Go as fast as you can and then come and tell me what it is like."

Some of the **children** set off by bicycle. Others went on

roller skates.   Still **others** travelled by go-cart.

Some went **flying**

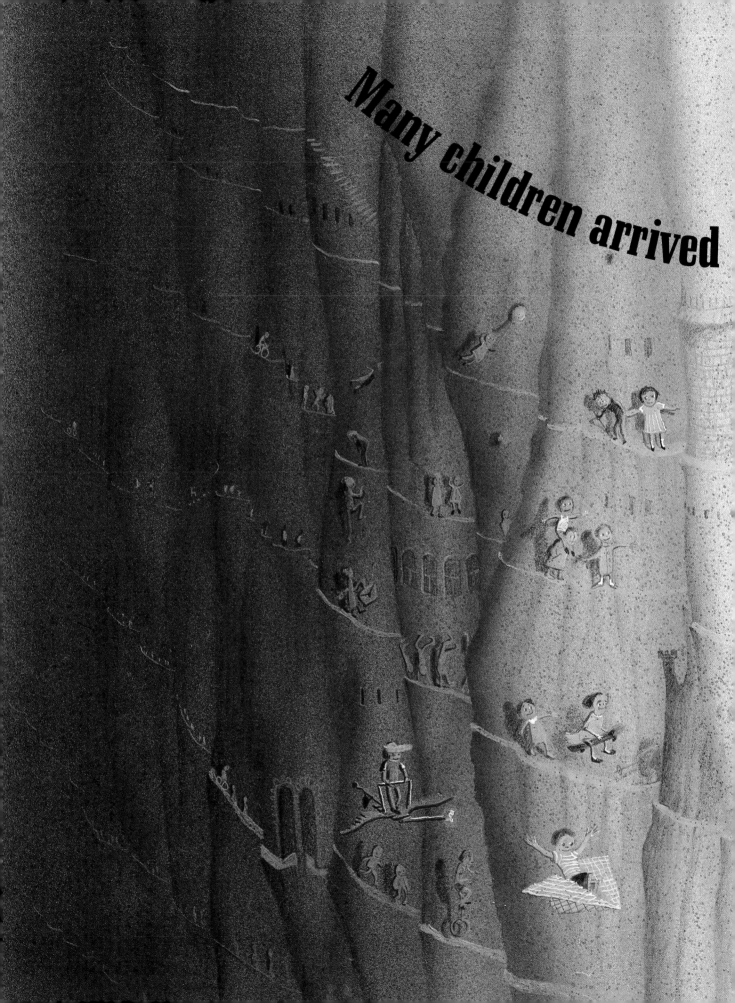

Many children arrived

at The **Other** Side quite soon,
while others took years to get there,

and were old when they **finally** did.

and told stories while waiting for the others.

When they had
thoroughly explored
everything, they returned

and told the king,
"On The Other Side,
everything is just the
same as here, except it's

sb**1**ɒwʞɔɒd

They all reported
the same thing.

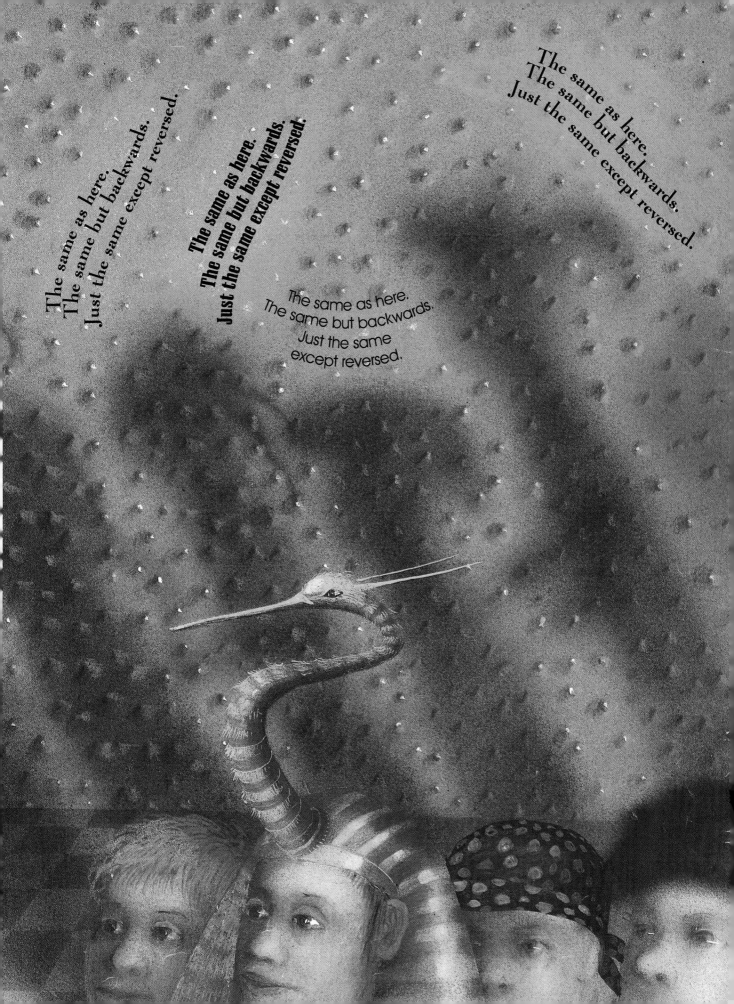

The same as here.
The same but backwards.
Just the same except reversed.

The same as here.
The same but backwards.
Just the same except reversed.

The same as here.
The same but backwards.
Just the same except reversed.

The same as here.
The same but backwards.
Just the same
except reversed.

"I want to go there!

Carry me,"

cried the king.

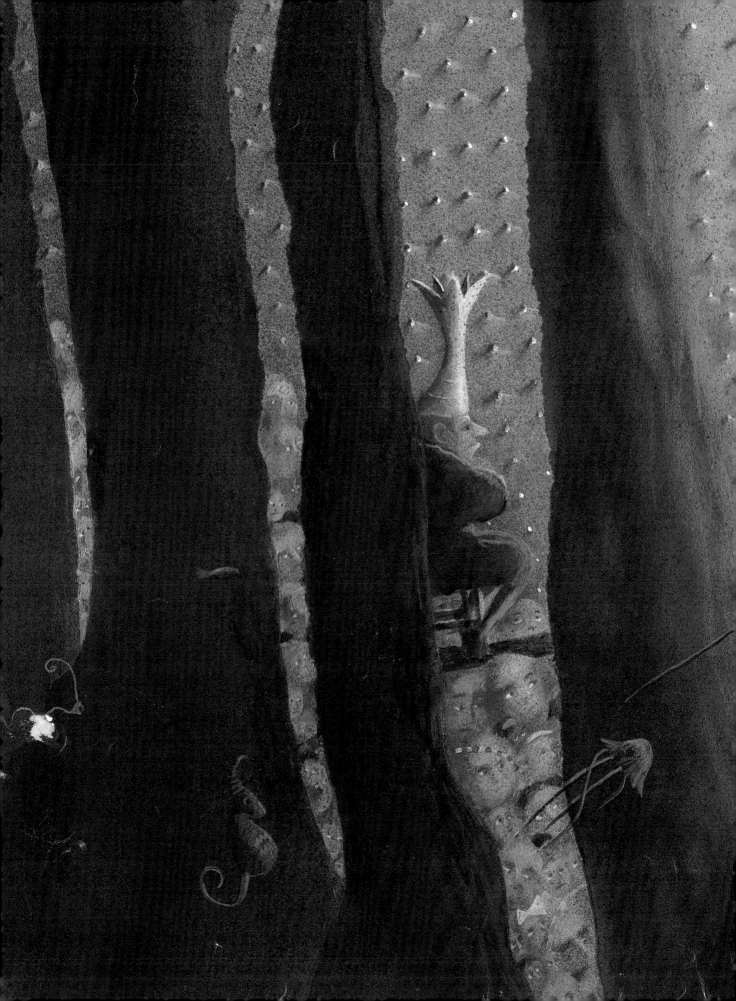

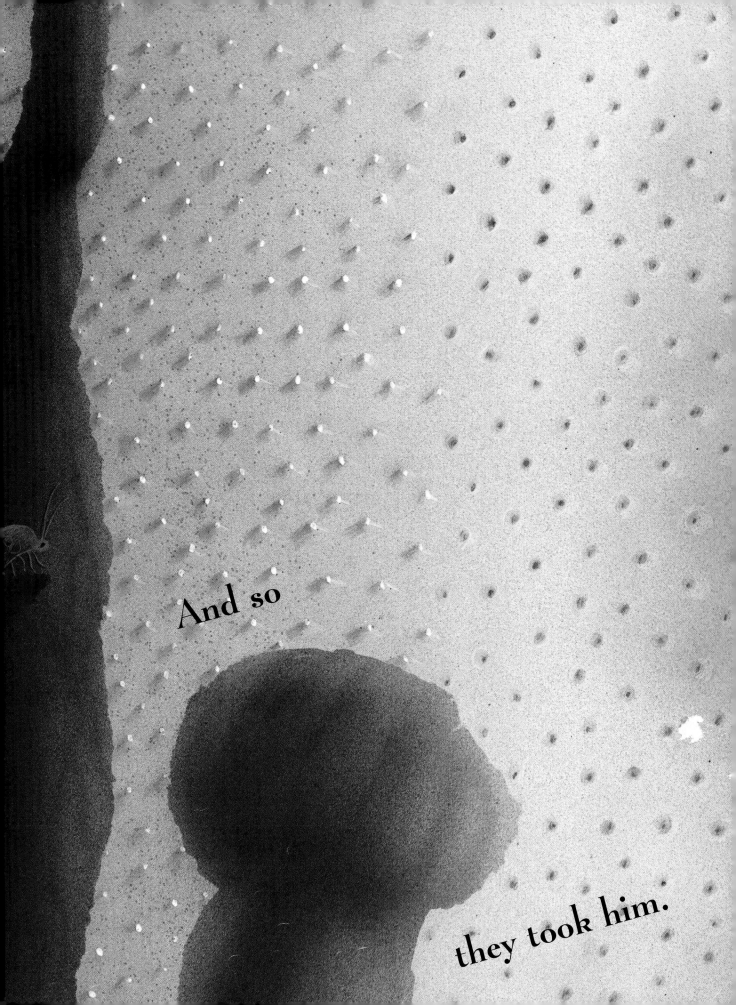

And so

they took him.

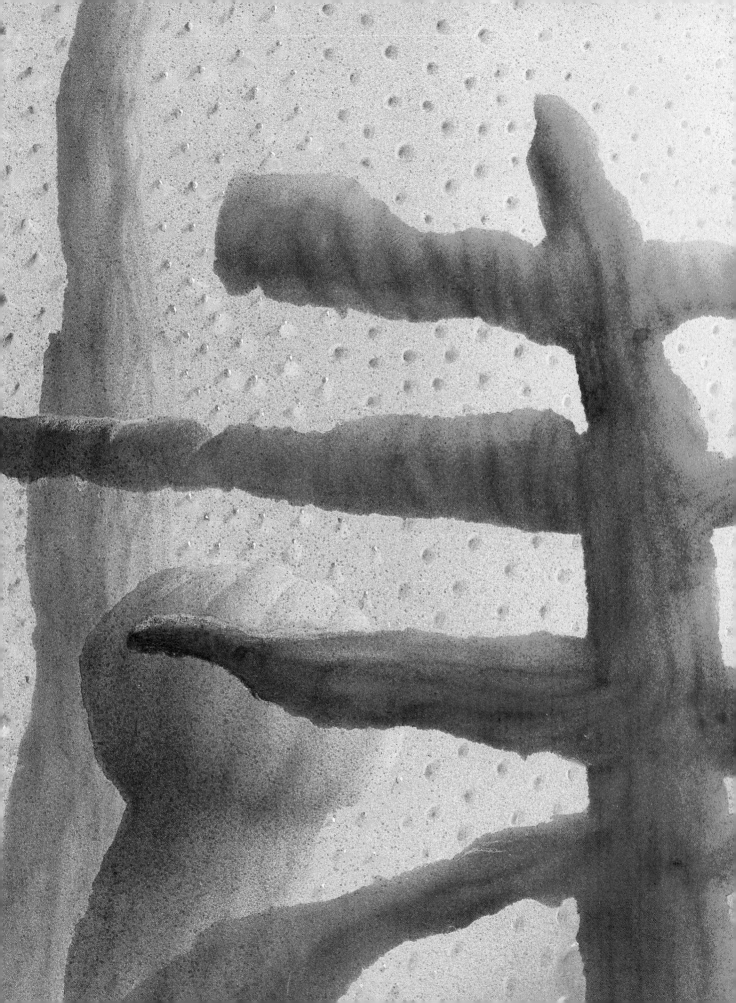

But when they had passed over to The **Other** Side,

the king had to carry **them,**
and he didn't like that **one** little **bit.**

So he demanded that they take him back,
but because **EVERYTHING** was backwards

And so they continued

until the **end** of time